The Spyglass

A Story of Faith

BY RICHARD PAUL EVANS

ILLUSTRATIONS BY JONATHAN LINTON

Simon & Schuster Books for Young Readers

NEW YORK LONDON TORONTO SYDNEY SINGAPORE

It is a privilege to create another book with my talented (and long suffering) friend, Jonathan Linton. I am grateful to again be working with
Ann Brashares (equally long suffering) and Les Morgenstein, as well as all the folks from Simon & Schuster Books for Young Readers,
especially Brenda Bowen and Steve Geck. I also thank Brian Tweede for his eye. And, as always, thank you Laurie L. I am pleased
to note that The Christmas Box House—the recipient of all my proceeds from this book—is operating and serving
hundreds of children each month. Most important, I thank my Heavenly Father, the source of all virtue.
—R. P. E.

I wish to thank the many people who helped with this project, especially Rick Evans for his faith in me. My special thanks to Ann Brashares for her patience in
being my liaison and Chelsey Rees Shipp for being a wonderful assistant. To my great models, Rick, Tawna, Lisa, Brandi, Judy, Jennifer, Barry, Jed, Alisha, Sean,
Annie, Olivia, Pa Todd, Tom, and Brother Jones. To my supportive family, especially my mom and dad. To my best friend and wife, Julie.
—J. M. L.

SIMON & SCHUSTER BOOKS FOR YOUNG READERS
An imprint of Simon & Schuster Children's Publishing Division
1230 Avenue of the Americas, New York, New York 10020
Text copyright © 2000 by Richard Paul Evans
Illustrations copyright © 2000 by Jonathan Linton
All rights reserved including the right of reproduction in whole or in part in any form.
Simon and Schuster Books for Young Readers is a trademark of Simon and Schuster.
The text of this book is set in 15-pt. Weiss.
The illustrations are rendered in oil paint.
Printed in the United States of America
4 6 8 10 7 5 3

Library of Congress Cataloging-in-Publication Data
Evans, Richard Paul.
The spyglass / by Richard Paul Evans ; illustrations by Jonathan Linton.
p. cm.
Summary: The inhabitants of a kingdom that has fallen on hard times discover the value
of faith when they learn to consider that which might be and labor to make it so.
ISBN 0-689-83466-7
[1. Faith—Fiction. 2. Kings, queens, rulers, etc.—Fiction.] I. Linton, Jonathan, ill. II. Title.
PZ7.E8923 Sp 2000
[Fic]—dc21
00-056978

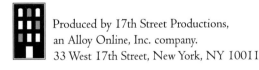

Produced by 17th Street Productions,
an Alloy Online, Inc. company.
33 West 17th Street, New York, NY 10011

To our handsome little man, Michael

—*R. P. E.*

To Julie

—*J. M. L.*

Once there was a great kingdom. This kingdom was known throughout all lands for its splendor: its magnificent buildings, its great, terraced gardens and bountiful farms. But through time, all that had changed. Now the once great buildings were falling down and in need of much repair. The farms were now small and did not grow enough food for the kingdom. The poor villagers would oftentimes go to bed hungry.

The people of this kingdom were not just poor by way of things, but they were poor of spirit—for there was not much joy in the village. There were no dances around the maypole nor palace cotillions. Rarely was music heard but for the simple pluckings from the lute of a traveling minstrel, now and again. Worst of all, the people had forgotten why their kingdom was once great.

The king of this land did not look as you might expect a king to look, for he did not have a magnificent throne or flowing robes or a golden crown inlaid with precious gems. He was the king of a poor kingdom, so he looked quite ordinary and poor himself. His castle was always cold and in need of repair. He had but one manservant and one milkmaid. He did not entertain the kings of other lands, for he was greatly ashamed of his kingdom.

To the east of this unhappy land was a beautiful kingdom with great farms and glorious cathedrals and castles. There were lovely gardens adorned with fine sculptures and sparkling fountains. Night and day, the breeze from the city walls carried the most exquisite music and the enticing scents of perfume—myrrh, cassia, and cypress—as well as the smell of delicacies, for there was an abundance of food in the land. It made the people even more unhappy to look on the wealth of their neighbors, for despite their poverty, the people prided themselves on having once been a great kingdom.

The king did not often leave his castle, for he was weary of the complaints of his subjects. One day as he sat down to a meager dinner of bread, a slab of cheese, and boiled mutton, there came a knock at the castle door. The king's servant opened the door to find an old man with a large oak walking stick. The man wore a cap and a girdle and a coarse woolen tunic. A large cloak of skins was draped over his shoulders. He was carrying a leather canister, which hung from his shoulder by rawhide thongs.

"Hail," said the old man. "I am but passing through your kingdom to the village to the east. I am looking for an inn to spend the night."

The servant frowned. "This is not an inn. This is the king's castle."

The traveler looked around in surprise. "This is not much of a castle," he said.

"Aye," the servant agreed.

"Still, I am weary from my journey. I would like to rest here."

"You must inquire of my lord," the servant said.

"Lead me to him," said the old man.

The servant led the old man down a dark, cold hallway to the king's dining room. The king looked up from his meal as the man entered.

"You are the king of this land?" the old man asked.

"I am," the king replied.

"You do not look like a king."

The king frowned. "I am the king of a poor kingdom. Our farms do not grow, our buildings are falling down, and my people weary me day and night with their complaints. We were once a great kingdom, but all that has changed."

The old man nodded slowly. "Why do you not change back?" he asked.

"Change?" the king replied angrily. "We have tried, only to fail. We lack all knowledge of what once made this kingdom great."

"You lack but one thing," said the old man. "If you will give me supper and lodging for the night, I will, on the morrow, show you why you fail."

The king looked at him thoughtfully, then said, motioning to the platters of bread, cheese, and meat, "Eat your fill."

The servant brought in a wooden platter and the old man ate with the king. When the old man had finished his meal, the servant led him to a room. That night as the king lay in his bed he wondered if the stranger had tricked him.

The next morning the old man came to the king in his throne room. "You have lived up to your part of the bargain. Now I will live up to mine. Follow me."

The king followed the old man to the castle balcony. There the old man brought out a long, round canister and pulled from it a brass tube with a sewn leather cover. A spyglass. He raised the spyglass to his eye and looked out over the land until a smile crossed his face. Then he handed the spyglass to the king. "Look thither."

The king looked out through the glass. He could see great farms and gardens, magnificent castles and cathedrals. He lowered the spyglass and said impatiently, "I have seen the wonders of the eastern kingdom. I hear far too much of them."

"You are mistaken," said the old man. "It is your own kingdom you see."

The king again raised the spyglass. This time he recognized the hills and glens of his own kingdom. But where there had been barren pasture there were now fields of grain stretching as far as the eye could see. His own people were in the fields, their wagons overflowing with their harvest.

"You are a wizard," said the king. "It is a trick of the glass."

"It is no trick," said the old man.

But when the king put down the glass his kingdom looked the same as before. "Nothing has changed."

"No," said the old man. "Change requires work. But one must first see before doing."

The king again raised the glass. "What greatness this kingdom holds."

"You have seen what might be," said the old man. "Now go and make it so. After two harvests I will return for my spyglass."

The king, on horseback, went out into his kingdom. He rode until he came to the edge of a once beautiful garden, now overrun with weeds and thistles. No one walked in the garden. There was neither the happy cries of playing children nor the pleased sighs of lovers. A group of villagers were standing outside its fence. Their children played at their feet in the dirty roadway.

"Why do you not use the garden?" the king asked them.

"It is not fit, sire," replied a woman.

"So it is not," agreed the king. "But it could be. Look." The king held out the spyglass. One by one the villagers looked through the tube at the garden. The weeds and thistles were gone and the lawns were lush and inviting. But when they set down the glass the garden had returned to its overgrown state.

"It is an amusing device," said one man. "But of no use."

"No use indeed," the king said. "Behold, knave." And he went to the garden and began to pull the weeds up by his own hand. When the villagers saw what he was doing, they too began to pull up weeds until they had uncovered a large, marble statue of an angel, its wings spread, its face looking toward heaven. The people stared at the statue in silent awe.

At length the king mounted his horse. Before he left he said, "You have seen what might be. Now make it so."

The king rode farther down the road until he came to a farmer sitting on the ground threshing grain with a small flail.

"How goes it, man?" the king asked.

The weary farmer barely looked up. "Can't grow e'en enough to feed ourselves, sire," the farmer sadly replied.

The king lifted the spyglass from his coat. "Come hither, good man. Behold your farm."

The farmer lifted the eyepiece to his eye and gasped. "It is sorcery."

"You have seen what might be," said the king. "Now make it so."

Farther down the road the king came to a crumbling cathedral. The roof had rotted and fallen in, and it was no longer safe to enter its arched doors. There were tents pitched outside, where a small congregation had gathered. The king rode his horse up to the tent. The friar who stood before the people stopped speaking at his approach. All turned to see the king.

"Why do you meet in tents?" the king asked.

"Why, sire, our cathedral has fallen."

"Why have you not rebuilt it?"

The friar opened his arms to his congregation. "We are few in number and poor."

"Have you shown your congregation what could be?" the king asked.

The friar looked quizzically at the king. "And what might that be?"

"See for yourself," said the king, handing him the spyglass. The friar looked through it and saw a new cathedral, larger than the decaying building and more elaborate, adorned with beautiful sculptures of saints and cherubs. The friar stared in awe. "By the grace of God," he said, "I have seen a vision."

"You have seen what might be," said the king. "Now make it so."

Day by day the king went out until he had visited all the people of his kingdom and shown them what might be. Though there were those who would not look through the glass or who refused to believe what they saw, the greater part of the villagers looked with wonder and hope.

That same year there was a plentiful harvest and the farmers filled their wagons and barns with grain. But not just the farmers prospered. The wagon builders were busy building wagons to carry all the grain. The millers were busy milling the grain into flour. For the first time, for as long as the villagers could remember, there was more than enough to eat. Music and dancing again filled the streets. Old buildings were repaired and new buildings arose, including the beginning of the most majestic cathedral in all the land.

As promised, two harvests later the old man returned to the kingdom. He almost did not recognize the castle, for so greatly had it changed. The scarred wooden door he had once knocked on was new and intricately carved. Beautiful tapestries adorned the now polished marble floors. The castle's once cold chambers were warmed with heat and music, and the king was attended to by a bevy of servants and maids. The king, dressed in lavish robes of fur and silk, warmly welcomed the old man.

"My friend," he said, "I have awaited your return. Look what prosperity your spyglass has brought my people. Let us make merry and prepare a great feast in your honor."

The old man smiled. "You have done well," he said. "But I cannot tarry. I have only come for my spyglass, then I will be on my way."

At this the king frowned. "In the two seasons since you blessed us with your arrival we have accumulated much treasure. In exchange for the spyglass, I will trade all the gold in the royal coffers, with men and wagons enough to carry it to wherever your destination."

"You have spoken wisely," said the old man, "for the gift of the spyglass is worth more than all the gold in all the royal coffers all throughout the land. But keep your gold. You no longer need the spyglass."

"But there is still much to be done," pleaded the king.

"Yes," said the old man. "But you no longer need the spyglass. You can see without it."

"How is it possible?" asked the king.

"The spyglass only showed you what could be if you believed, for it was only faith that you and your people lacked."

The king shook his head in disbelief. "How can this be? Faith is foolishness."

"So says the fool," the old man said. "Faith is the beginning of all journeys. It is by faith that the seed is planted. It is by faith that the foundation is dug. It is by faith that each book is penned and each song is written. Only with faith can we see that which is not, but can be. The eye of faith is greater than the natural eye, for the natural eye sees only a portion of truth. The eye of faith sees without bounds or limits."

"I had not supposed," the king said.

"That is why you once failed," said the old man. "Faith is why you now succeed." He placed his hand on the king's shoulder and said with a smile, "You have seen what might be. Now go and make it so."

And though the old man and his spyglass were never again seen in the land, the kingdom continued to prosper and became again the great kingdom of old. Yet, despite their abundance of food, their beautiful buildings, their lush gardens and majestic cathedrals, it was ever after said of that kingdom that their greatest treasure was their faith.

What is the most important thing we can do for our at-risk children?

In 1996, Richard and Keri Evans sponsored a children's welfare conference to discuss this question. The answer was to create The Christmas Box House International, an organization dedicated to helping abused and neglected children by building special shelter/assessment facilities. The Christmas Box House is a one-stop shelter and assessment facility for abused and neglected children—children who are currently shuffled from agency to agency, from police officer to doctor to caseworker, before being thrust into a new home. At The Christmas Box House all these visits occur on-site, providing familiarity and comfort at a difficult time. In addition, The Christmas Box House brings together child advocates, including foster families, Children's Advocacy Centers, the Center for Children's Justice, and government agencies, to provide and enhance services for at-risk children.

For more information about The Christmas Box House, or to make a contribution, please visit our Web site at:

www.richardpaulevans.com

or write to us at:

Richard Paul Evans
P.O. Box 1416
Salt Lake City, Utah 84110